TEAM SPIRIT

by Lucinda Cotter
illustrated by Joseph Wilkins

a Capstone company — publishers for children

Engage Literacy is published in the UK by Raintree.
Raintree is an imprint of Capstone Global Library Limited, a company incorporated in England and Wales
having its registered office at 264 Banbury Road, Oxford, OX2 7DY – Registered company number: 6695582

www.raintree.co.uk

Illustration copyright Capstone/Joseph Wilkins

Editorial credits
Jennifer Huston, editor; Richard Parker, designer; Katy LaVigne, production specialist

10 9 8 7 6 5 4 3 2 1
Printed and bound in China.

Team Spirit

ISBN: 978 1 4747 3926 9

Contents

Chapter 1
LET'S PLAY!

"Come on Budford!" yelled Coach Robin from the side of the football pitch.

Lily stood in the middle of the pitch,
ready to kick the ball.
The other team, Ilminster Girls,
had just scored a goal.
Lily's team was losing, and the game
was almost over.

Lily stood very still, smoothed her navy shirt, and then kicked the ball.

It flew down the pitch towards Lily's teammate, but she wasn't watching.

A player from Ilminster Girls stopped the ball with her foot.

She kicked it and sent it flying the other way.

Lily ran as fast as she could.
But the Ilminster Girls quickly passed the ball
from one player to another towards their goal.
Ilminster Girls made it look so easy.
And Lily's teammates didn't even seem
to be trying to take the ball away from them.

When Emma got the ball, Lily thought
there might still be a chance
to score a goal.
"Emma, I'm over here!" she called.
"Pass it to me!"

Emma just stood there, not sure what to do.
Then a player from Ilminster Girls rushed in
and got the ball away from her.

Lily watched as an Ilminster Girls player
dribbled the ball down the pitch.
Then the player kicked it towards the goal.
It all seemed to happen very slowly.
The goalkeeper for Budford Girls
was talking to another player
instead of watching the game.
She saw the ball too late.

It soared over her head, just as the referee
blew his whistle to end the match.
It was another goal for Ilminster Girls
and another loss for Budford Girls.

"Oh, no," groaned Lily.
"Our team is hopeless," she thought
to herself.

Chapter 2
A DREAM WIN

"We haven't won a game all season," complained Lily at the dinner table. "Nobody is trying at all."

"What does Coach Robin have to say about it?" asked Mum.

"She tries to help us, but nobody listens," replied Lily.
She pushed her food around on her plate. She wasn't feeling very hungry.

"But *you* listen," said Dad.

"Yes, but sometimes it feels like
I'm the only one who even wants to play,"
said Lily angrily.
She put her fork down and pushed
her plate away.
"We're just not having fun anymore."

That night Lily had a dream.

In the dream she was playing with her favourite team, Tilbury United.

They were playing in a big-league game.

She kicked the winning goal.

Then the Tilbury United players carried her off the pitch on their shoulders.

In the morning, Lily had an idea.
First she told Mum and Dad.
Then they spoke to Coach Robin.
They sent some emails and made
some phone calls.
A few days later at practice,
Lily had a surprise for her teammates.

Chapter 3
STRIKERS AND TILBURY

When Lily and the others turned up
for practice, there were some new players
on the pitch.

Coach Robin had a huge smile on her face.
"I'd like you all to meet some special guests,"
she said.
"We're very lucky to have Kate and Jasmine
from Tilbury United here today,
as well as Tyler and Zach from the Strikers.
They will be training you this afternoon."

Lily looked around at the other girls.
They were all listening now!

"Who's ready to play some football?"
asked Jasmine.

It was the best practice they had ever had!
The big-league players went through
all the skills with the team.
Soon everyone was trying their best
and having lots of fun.
There was plenty of laughter
and even more huffing and puffing.

After practice the guests showed the girls
their own skills.
Lily was amazed by what they could do.
It was easy to see how they had
made it to the big leagues.
She hoped that one day she would play
as well as Kate and Jasmine.

Chapter 4
GO BUDFORD!

The next Saturday was match day.
As Lily stood on the pitch, she gazed around
at her team.
The referee blew his whistle,
and the match began.

A player from the other team kicked the ball
to a teammate.
Then she passed it to another player
who gave it a huge kick.
The ball went flying towards the goal.
"Here we go again," thought Lily.

But this time, the Budford Girls' goalkeeper
was ready.
She stepped in front of the ball,
and it bounced off her chest.
Then she stopped the ball with her foot
and quickly passed it to Emma.

Emma kicked the ball back up the pitch.
Rani was waiting for the ball so she could
pass it to Lin.

Lin dribbled the ball around a player
from the other team.
Then she kicked it towards the goal.
The goalkeeper reached up to grab the ball,
but it flew over her head and landed
in the net.
Everyone on the Budford team cheered.
Lily was so excited.

Finally, her team had a chance of winning!
After that, the game got really exciting.
Both teams worked hard to get the ball.
It raced from one end of the pitch
to the other.

On the side of the pitch, Coach Robin
cheered with a huge smile on her face.

When the other team scored a goal to win
the match, Lily didn't even mind.
"At least now our players are having fun
and trying to win," she thought, smiling.